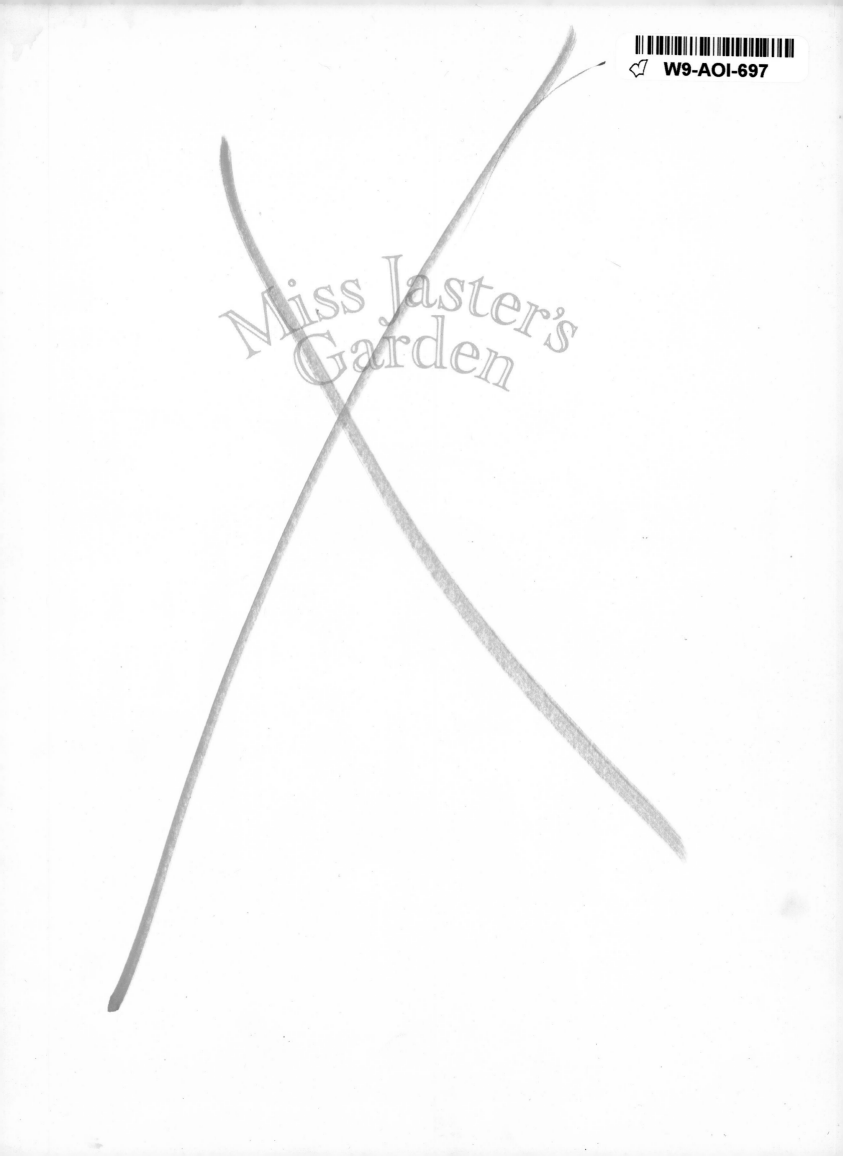

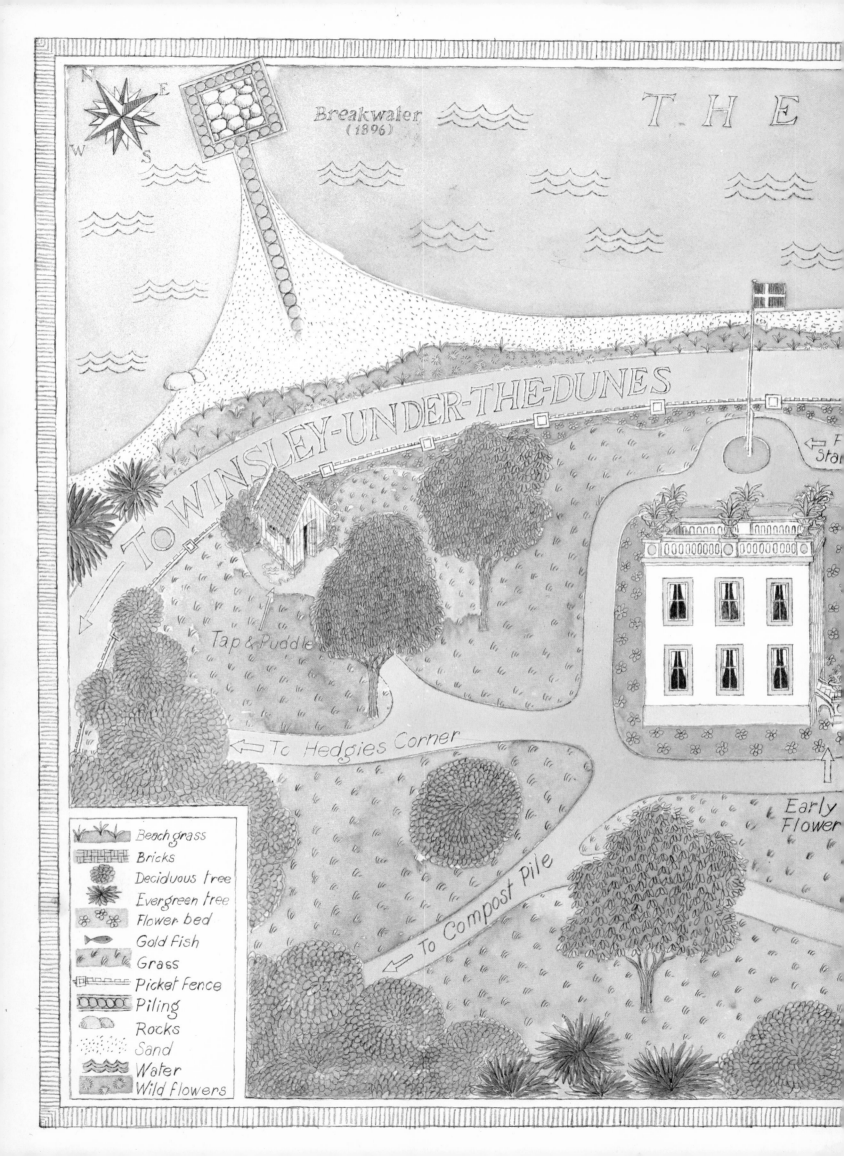

SEA

To Sandgate

Stairs to Beach

Sunrise Hill
(Elevation 9')

Stairs to Hill

Front Gate

Miss J's Wicker Chair

The Junipers

Bird Bath
(For ancient inscription see page: 11)

Fish Pond
(Depth 2'3")

Sundial

Mulberry Tree

Plan of
MISS JASTER'S
GARDEN
Sandgate-On-Sea
Scale: 1:100
Prepared for
The Royal Horticultural Survey
Mullwich

To
Mrs. Sinclair

Miss Jaster's Garden

by N. M. Bodecker

 GOLDEN PRESS · NEW YORK
WESTERN PUBLISHING COMPANY, INC.
RACINE, WISCONSIN

In a corner of a garden, overlooking the sea at Sandgate, lived a small spiky animal called a Hedgehog, Hedgie for short.

In the middle of the garden lived Miss Jaster in "Villa Pax," a square, whitewashed house with ornamental flowerpots on the front steps.

The two did not see much of each other, because Hedgie was by nature nocturnal, and Miss Jaster was not. But occasionally they met, just after sunset, when they both enjoyed strolling in the garden.

On these occasions, Miss Jaster would go back into the house and return a few minutes later with a saucer of milk, which she placed at what she hoped was the right end of the hedgehog. But hedgehogs

being the shape they are, and Miss Jaster being a little nearsighted, as often as not she put the saucer where the hedgehog's head wasn't. And Hedgie — so as not to cause distress — politely dipped his tail in the milk and pretended to drink. Later, when Miss Jaster went into the house and lit the lamp on the piano, he drank the milk properly.

Through the open door he could hear Miss Jaster at the piano, her fingers fluttering up and down the keyboard, picking out little tunes as sweet and unpredictable as April showers.

Hedgie liked being played for while he had his milk, and Miss Jaster enjoyed having someone to play for.

This way they lived happily for a while.

Then one bright May morning, when the air was soft and full of birdsong, Miss Jaster came into the garden to do her spring planting.

She wore a purple morning-dress and sturdy shoes. She had a large straw hat, trimmed with cornflowers, on her head, and pulled behind her a small, four-wheeled wagon full of garden tools and envelopes of flower seeds. She carried a large, green watering can with the letters J.J. (for Jessica Jaster) painted on it in blue. And because the sun was bright, and because her eyes were a little watery from reading planting instructions, she wore her dark glasses.

These glasses made everything look brownish-gray, the same color as the empty flower bed she was about to seed, and the same color as Hedgie, who was asleep in the middle of it.

The flower bed was on the south side of the house, a protected nook, out of the wind, and full of sun. It was the first spot Miss Jaster planted each spring.

She raked the bed lightly with a small rake. She sprinkled the seeds evenly: Marigold and Baby's Breath and patches of Sweet

William. She showered it all generously with her watering can, never suspecting that a small, spiky animal was in the middle of it.

At first Hedgie thought of moving to a safer spot, but his quills did need combing, and he rather enjoyed having his back scratched. So he stayed.

He hardly felt the seeds at all; they were like dust settling among his quills.

As for the shower from the watering can, it was like a gentle rain —not at all unpleasant after the heat and the dust.

When Miss Jaster went into the house to have lunch, Hedgie went back to sleep, enjoying the most perfect dreams.

Every day after that, Miss Jaster came with her watering can to sprinkle the flower bed and watch for green shoots.

And every night, Hedgie wandered through the garden, sniffing and nibbling the way Hedgehogs do.

But after a while he began feeling restless. Something was happening, he didn't know what, but deep down among his quills, something was stirring and squirming, like a thousand tiny fingers touching and tickling his skin. He was so itchy he couldn't sleep, and so curious he had to know just what was wrong.

Down by the tool shed, where Miss Jaster filled her watering can in the afternoon, was a small puddle of clear water, for the tap was worn and kept dripping. Hedgie used it as his mirror, and down to this mirror he went to have a look at himself. But when he got there, and leaned over the puddle, he stood quite still for several moments, curling and uncurling his toes in disbelief: what he saw in the water was not his ordinary, gray-brown, prickly self, but something quite, quite different.

Peeping out from among his quills were little spikes and shoots of green, some with leaves and some with tendrils, ready to climb and bloom and fill with bees and honey.

"Well," he said to himself, "now I'm either a flower bed or a vegetable garden. I wonder which?" And he kept looking at himself and wondering, till another drop from the tap broke the picture into a thousand pieces.

When Miss Jaster came with her watering can that evening, Hedgie was back in his old spot, and the whole flower bed was full of little spikes and shoots of green.

So pleased was Miss Jaster, that she played the entire "Blue Danube Waltz" on her piano, twice over, before going to bed.

But Hedgie was only half listening. "Flower bed or vegetable garden? Vegetable garden or flower bed?" he kept saying to himself. "Which am I? I wonder."

The fact was, that during the day he had had the most alarming dreams.

First he dreamt that he was covered with tomato plants. One by one the tomatoes ripened and dropped off the vine, squashing on his head, ripping on his quills, till he looked as if he were covered by tomato sauce. Then the vines changed. They grew longer and heavier, trailing twenty feet behind him, covered with large yellow flowers. "Melon-flowers," thought Hedgie.

And in his dreams the flowers turned into huge, ripe melons—dozens of them, dragging behind and growing, till he could not move another step.

At that moment he woke up. All over him and around him were growing plants. If only he could be sure they were not tomatoes or melons.

Early the next morning, he went down to the tool shed, nosing about under the tables, among the flowerpots, till he found the seed packs, half hidden under Miss Jaster's garden gloves. A few seeds were left in each, so Miss Jaster had kept them for use later in the summer.

Hedgie pulled the packs out on the floor in front of him: Marigolds and Baby's Breath and fragrant Sweet William. He did not know their names, but he did recognize the pictures on the packs.

They were neither tomatoes nor melons! Much relieved, he went to have a look at himself in the puddle.

"I believe I shall be quite handsome," he said, and toddled off to bed.

15

Not many days after this, Hedgie woke up early in the afternoon, feeling the presence of a strange, new something that hadn't been there the day before.

It wasn't exactly a sound, and it wasn't exactly a touch; it wasn't really a taste, and it certainly wasn't a sight, for his eyes were tightly closed.

For a while he lay quite still, wiggling his nose and sniffing. . . .

"It's a smell," he thought at last, "but a smell with something else in it: a hum of bees—a touch of sun and—"

And when he opened his eyes, the flowers were all around him: Marigolds and Baby's Breath and patches of Sweet William.

"I'm in bloom!" cried Hedgie, and hurried down to the tool shed to look at himself.

But no matter how long he looked, or how hard he tried, he could find only one word to describe what he saw: Stupendous! (And even that was not really the word he wanted.)

While he stood there in the sunshine, a little dazed, not knowing what to do next, a small cloud of butterflies and bees gathered around him, fluttering and humming.

Hedgie didn't mind. He was not afraid of bees. "After all, a bee has only one stinger," he thought, "but I have over two hundred."

And whoever ever heard of anyone being afraid of butterflies?

But Hedgie wasn't really thinking of the hum and flutter around him. Something inside him was fluttering and humming, bursting to get out: the special kind of whatever-it-is that makes birds sing, and poets make poetry, and puppy dogs chase their tails.

While he was thinking this, his feet began doing little dance steps in the dust, all on their own. One moment they looked as if they were waltzing; the next moment they were doing a tap dance! Then a skip and a jump, then a slow turn 'round the puddle.

"Oh it cannot be helped—" thought Hedgie as he waltzed into the flower bed.

"I really shouldn't do this—" he said as he jumped over the Marigolds.

"But I absolutely must!" he cried as he burst onto the lawn, skipping and jumping and kicking his heels.

Around the fishpond he raced, under the garden seat and into the sun. Behind him trailed the bees and butterflies like a noisy cloud of flower petals.

"Tomorrow I'll be as quiet as an earthworm," thought Hedgie, "but not today. Today is the greatest day in my life. There'll never be another like it!"

And the bees and the butterflies, tired of chasing their food around the lawn, hoped he was right.

Miss Jaster had been dozing in her wicker chair, when she saw—or believed she saw—a small patch of her flower bed jump onto the lawn and head for the gate.

At first she thought it was a dream, but when she found that she was quite awake, she said the first thing that came into her head:

"Stop thief!" she called, and then, at the top of her voice: "STOP THIEF!"

In a flash Hedgie saw that she was right. The flowers were hers, not his. Taking them out of the flower bed—even if it was only to perform a midsummer dance around the fishpond—really made him a kind of thief.

If only Miss Jaster had remained in her chair, Hedgie would have gone back to his place in the flower bed, much chastened.

But she jumped up, waving her parasol, and poor Hedgie, now quite frightened, dashed through the gate and down the road to the village.

In a small cloud of dust, many yards behind, came Miss Jaster, her knitting, her parasol, and her cries for help!

Then up the road from the village came the police constable on his bicycle, making what speed he could uphill toward Miss Jaster, carrying a parcel to his sister in Winsley.

For Hedgie there was only one thing left to do. He scurried in among the wildflowers at the roadside, and lay stock-still, hoping he would not be seen.

Half an hour later, Wimple the Constable handed Miss Jaster her knitting over the garden gate. After much listening on the dusty road, he at last understood, or believed he understood, what had happened.

"I quite understand, Miss," he said, taking off his helmet and wiping his forehead. "But one last question please: Did you, by any chance, happen to notice how many legs these flowers had, when they made their getaway? In round numbers."

Miss Jaster tucked the knitting under her arm and straightened her straw hat. "A great many, Constable," she said firmly. "A great many!"

Wimple licked his pencil, and added to his description of the fugitive. "Legs:" he wrote, "numerous!"

"Very good, Miss," he said, "we'll have your Zinnias back in no time at all."

"Marigolds," said Miss Jaster, and went into her garden.

"Of course," said Wimple, and moved off down the road.

In the sixteen years he had been in Sandgate-on-Sea, no one had ever reported a missing flower bed.

"Sometimes the kids pick a few plums or apples that aren't exactly theirs," he thought. "And sometimes, I suppose, they pick a few flowers that strictly speaking belong to someone else. Well. But when flower beds start running off on their own—" Wimple shook his head sadly. "And there's another thing," he thought, "how do you punish a flower bed? Or a watermelon?"

The Constable stopped in the middle of the road, and put his helmet back on. It was a very hot day.

He tried to decide how he should begin. "Put yourself in the fugitive's place," the Chief Constable always said. "Imagine *you* were running away. Where would *you* hide?"

"If I were a flower," thought Wimple. "A flower?" He could imagine himself being a cabbage or a melon, and for some reason, even an artichoke, but a flower?

He looked around him. Where would a flower — "Of course," he said, slapping his hand against his helmet, "that's where I should hide. Among the other flowers!"

He straightened himself up, brushed a little dust off his sleeve, and started down the road, poking among the weeds and wildflowers, looking for Marigolds, and Baby's Breath, and a patch of Sweet William.

But it was nearly sunset, two days later, before he brought Hedgie back to "Villa Pax." On a leash.

Never in his life had Hedgie felt so sad, so tired, and so hopelessly small.

His feet were sore, his flowers had wilted. He was a weary, worried, bedraggled little animal, down on his luck.

"Goodness sakes!" said Miss Jaster. "It's the Hedgehog!"

"Flowerhog's more like it," said Wimple. But Miss Jaster had already gone into the house. Presently she came back, with a saucer of milk.

This time she took no chance, but knelt down, right there on the garden steps, and put the milk in front of Hedgie. She was quite sure this time, for she saw his eyes, like two tiny drops of India ink in the fur. And they were looking straight into her own.

Miss Jaster had to clear her throat twice before asking the Constable to get the watering can.

A little later, freed from the leash, and fed and showered, Hedgie toddled back to his flower bed.

The Constable, having enjoyed a little homemade gooseberry wine and a chat about annual borders, returned to the village.

Miss Jaster lit the lamp on her piano, but tonight her heart was not in the "Blue Danube Waltz." She kept thinking of the friendly little flowerhog, and the frightful scare she must have given him.

After a while she turned off the lamp and sat looking into the garden, till the moon rose behind the junipers.

Early the next morning Hedgie met Miss Jaster on the front steps; she was carrying a tray with her own breakfast and Hedgie's milk.

That morning (and many mornings after) they had breakfast together by the fishpond, Miss Jaster in her wicker chair, Hedgie in the grass.

After a leisurely breakfast they went for a walk along the beach, followed by a small but persistent butterfly.

At the end of the breakwater they sat down, Miss Jaster dangling her feet in the water, Hedgie resting his nose on his paws.

And there was nothing but peace and sunshine and a touch of Sweet William.

Breakwater
(1896)

T H E

To WINSLEY-UNDER-THE-DUNES

Tap & Puddle

← To Hedgies Corner

To Compost Pile

Sta

Early
Flower

Legend:
- Beach grass
- Bricks
- Deciduous tree
- Evergreen tree
- Flower bed
- Gold fish
- Grass
- Picket fence
- Piling
- Rocks
- Sand
- Water
- Wild flowers

SEA

Stairs to
Beach →

TO SANDGATE

Sunrise Hill →
(Elevation 9')

Front Gate

Stairs
to Hill ⇐

Miss J's
Wicker
Chair →

Bird Bath
(For ancient inscription
see page : 11)

The Junipers
→

← Fish Pond
(Depth 2'3")

← Sundial

← Mulberry Tree

Plan of
MISS JASTER'S
GARDEN
Sandgate-On-Sea
Scale: 1:100
Prepared for
The Royal Horticultural Survey
Mullwich